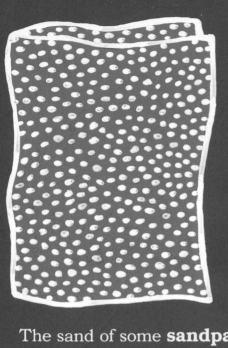

Because a **hammer** has so
many uses, including making
other tools, it is sometimes
called the "king of tools."

The sand of some **sandpaper**
is made of ground-up garnets,
red semiprecious stones.

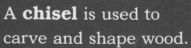

A **chisel** is used to
carve and shape wood.

To Kevin Toupin,
a great neighbor, gardener,
and builder of birdhouses
—P.S.

Hugs to Philemon
—S.H.

I Love Tools!
Text copyright © 2006 by Philemon Sturges
Illustrations copyright © 2006 by Shari Halpern
Manufactured in China.
All rights reserved.
www.harperchildrens.com

Library of Congress Cataloging-in-Publication Data
Sturges, Philemon.
I love tools! / by Philemon Sturges ;
illustrated by Shari Halpern.—1st ed.   p.   cm.
Summary: A boy and girl use a variety of tools to make a
house for a friendly bluebird.
ISBN-10: 0-06-009287-4 — ISBN-10: 0-06-009288-2 (lib. bdg.)
ISBN-13: 978-0-06-009287-0
ISBN-13: 978-0-06-009288-7 (lib. bdg.)
[1. Tools—Fiction. 2. Birdhouses—Fiction.
3. Stories in Rhyme.]
I. Halpern, Shari, ill.   II. Title.
PZ8.3.S9227Iadw   2006   [E]—dc22   2004029891

1 2 3 4 5 6 7 8 9 10
❖
First Edition

I Love Tools!

BY **Philemon Sturges**

ILLUSTRATED BY **Shari Halpern**

📚 **HarperCollins** *Publishers*

Tools, tools, tools! I like tools.

I love my ruler. I love my square.

They help us draw a straight line—there!

The sharp saw cuts the line,

and the sawdust smells like pine.

The hammer pounds a nail, and then—

The chisel makes
a groove or two.

The drill will drill a hole right through.

Why don't you spread
a dab of glue?

I'll twist the clamp.
I'll clean the ooze.

Let's make a perch the bird can use!

The screwdriver twists in the screws.

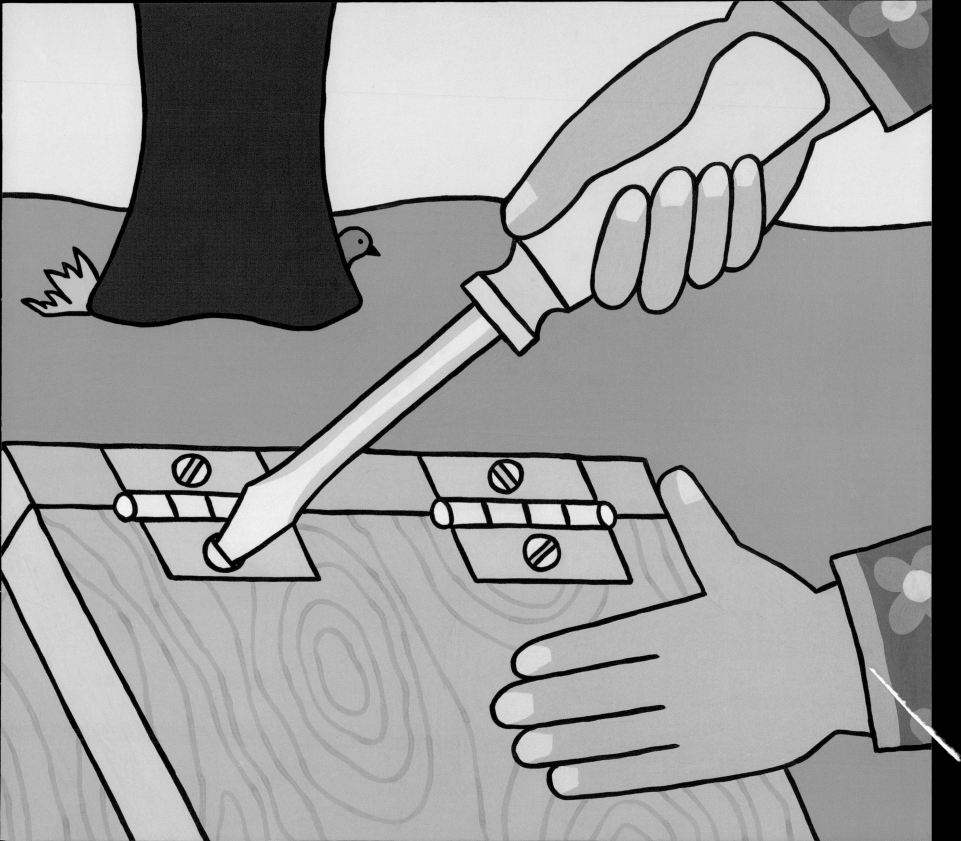

Sandpaper smoothes it neat and clean.

The paintbrush paints the outside green.
Let's stencil on a leafy scene!
Little bluebird, here's the best . . .

Place you'll ever build a nest!

Tools, tools, tools! I LOVE tools!

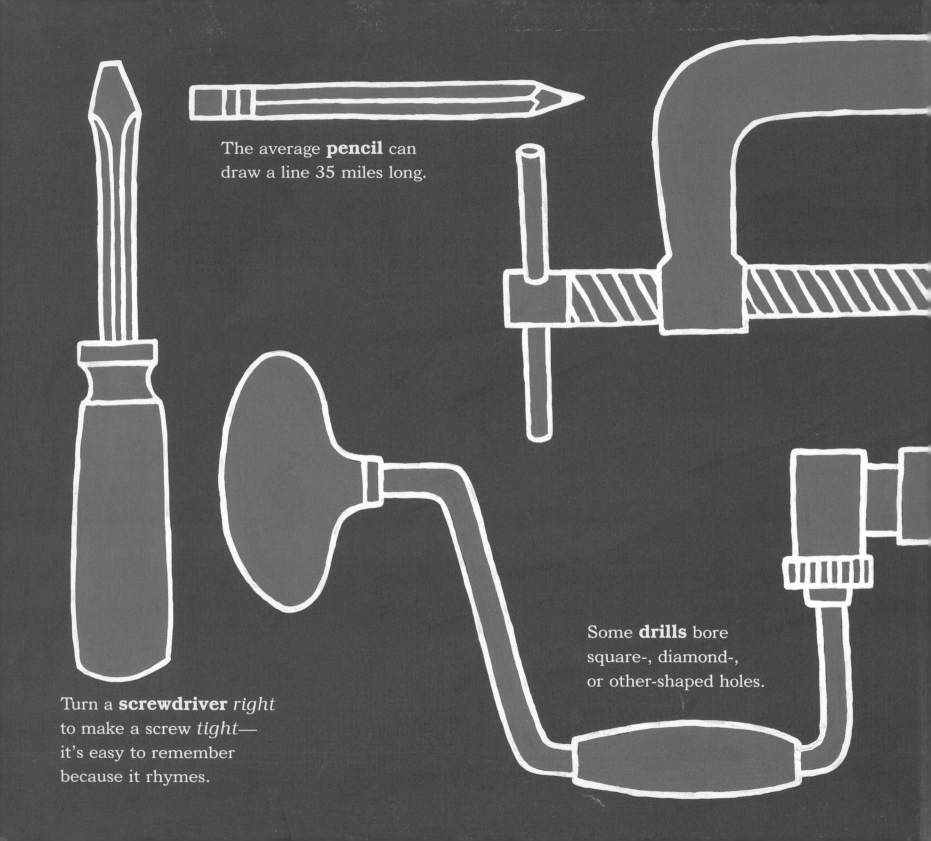

The average **pencil** can draw a line 35 miles long.

Turn a **screwdriver** *right* to make a screw *tight*— it's easy to remember because it rhymes.

Some **drills** bore square-, diamond-, or other-shaped holes.